About Leaf Books

Leaf Books' fine and upstanding mission is to support the publication of high quality short fiction, micro-fiction and poetry by both new and established writers.

We have put over 200 authors and poets into print since our inception in 2006. Many of them have never been published before.

See our website at www.leafbooks.co.uk for news, more information about our authors, other titles and having your own work published by Leaf.

Other Leaf Books Anthologies

The Better Craftsman and Other Stories
The Final Theory and Other Stories
Razzamatazz and Other Poems
Outbox and Other Poems
The Light That Remains and Other Short Stories
Dogstar and More Science Fiction Stories
Derek and More Micro-Fiction
Coffee and Chocolate
Naked Thighs and Cotton Frocks and Other Stories
The Someday Supplement
Imagine Coal and More Micro-Fiction
Standing on the Cast-Iron Shore and Other Poems

Discovering a Comet
and
More Micro-Fiction

First published by Leaf Books Ltd in 2008

www.leafbooks.co.uk

Leaf Books Ltd.
GTi Suite,
Valleys Innovation Centre,
Navigation Park,
Abercynon,
CF45 4SN

Printed by Jem
www.jem.co.uk

ISBN-10: 1-905599-46-3
ISBN-13: 978-1-905599-46-2

Contents

Introduction

Discovering a Comet and More Micro-Fiction gathers together the thirty-six winning entries from Leaf Books 2008 micro-fiction competition. The competition drew in a lot of worthwhile material, and there were quite a few stories that very nearly made the cut ... we've definitely seen more and more people getting the hang of the format as the years have passed. Thus our fourth micro-fiction collection – we're proper experts now – is a pleasingly varied bag. Though not in quality terms. They're all pretty much ace.

We've only space to mention a few of our favourites here, but rest assured the ones we don't mention are our favourites as well.

Maureen Gallagher's 'An African Plant Begins with a D' beguiled us with its excellent portrayal of aphasia-induced frustration that nonetheless didn't shun the inherent humour in the situation – crucially, the protagonist is privy to that humour, so it comes across as heartening and optimistic rather than cruel, and her sheer joy at happening upon the word for which she was searching creates a genuinely triumphant moment. It shows a real love of language.

'Bad Apples' by Karen Jones also pleased the team mightily – it's about a painter's inability to make a bowl of apples look like anything more than apples. People are easy; it's still life that doggedly lives up to its name. It's such a straightforward and cleanly realised premise with a hugely satisfying final line. Or there's 'Infested' by Stewart Tiley, a disconcerting portrait of an enigmatic breaking relationship from the point of view of a small child. Haunting stuff. Stays with you.

Moving towards the grand finale (that actually opens the book ... blame us there an ill-chosen phrase), the eponymous runner-up, 'Discovering a Comet', is a total delight and made the entire Leaf Team smile and thrust it under one another's noses and then just generally seethe a bit because we wished we'd written it ourselves. It's a quirky little exploration of how you might react if someone popped a tiny comet through your letterbox. It's not as though you don't need to think about that sort of thing. And mostly it's powerfully funny. The sheer understated mundanity and reserve of the imagined protagonist's reaction – 'Imagine the frustration of wandering around Homebase, accosting blank-faced assistants to ask, "Excuse me, do you sell humane traps for comets, by any chance?"' – goes down very well indeed.

The winning story is 'Jesse and Jesus' by Freda Love Smith, and a properly brilliant story it is too. It's a tight, beautifully structured (it has three distinct acts) piece about a deeply troubled man profoundly affected in more than one way by a dream he has of Jesus. In essence. But it takes very well to repeat readings as it doesn't give itself away entirely on first perusal – the story stood out not only for its compact structure and strikingly straightforward prose but also for its bold refusal to commit to a self-limiting, grounding sort of an answer – very aptly, seeing as its disturbed and disturbing protagonist's repeated motto is 'Learn to love the questions, baby'. It's a story that we felt the need to return to again and again, and we hope you feel the same.

Our thanks to all who entered.

The Stories

Freda Love Smith

Freda Love Smith is an American living in Nottingham. In the U.S. she played drums in rock bands such as The Blake Babies with Juliana Hatfield and The Mysteries of Life. Since relocating with her partner and children in 2006, she has turned her attention to writing fiction. She is a part-time student in Creative Writing at The University of Nottingham and is working on a novel.

Jesse and Jesus

Jesse walked around with a paperback copy of Rilke in his jacket pocket. *Letters to a Young Poet*. He'd quote from it: 'Learn to love the questions,' except he'd say, 'Learn to love the questions, baby,' as if it were his final answer.

He had a dream one night. He'd fallen asleep on the floor, fully dressed in a chequered shirt, all buttoned up, the shabby white jacket with the Rilke, and grey, belted trousers, and as he fell asleep his hands were crossed over his chest and he said over and over again to himself he said 'help help help help'.

The dream was of Jesus.

'I didn't ask for *you* to come,' said Jesse.

'I don't only come to people who ask for me,' said Jesus. Then Jesus told him he didn't have to take the world so hard.

'Your ancestors were beings of light,' he'd said.

Jesse told everybody in the house about that dream, and for a while he did seem lighter, and didn't always stay up all night drinking black coffee and listening to Black Flag.

If I could slow down the movement of time, I'd show you something in him, something in his spaces in between, that most people can't see. It's a flame. It might seem a risk, having a friend like Jesse, but friendship is always risky.

After the shooting he went to jail and then back into the main hospital with its white everything. Nobody had been seriously injured. Even when heavily medicated he never had that flatness some of us have all the time.

I said, 'Why the *hell*, Jesse?'

He said, 'Learn to love the questions, baby.'

Pauline Masurel

Pauline Masurel is a gardener and writer who lives in Bath. Her short fiction has been published in anthologies, online and broadcast on radio. She is writer in residence at Bloom & Curll bookshop in Bristol and a regular performer with the storytelling group Heads and Tales. More about her work can be found at her website www.unfurling.net. She is currently learning fire juggling and has an ambition to write a story so short that it cannot be read with the naked eye.

Discovering a Comet

Imagine this: coming downstairs on a winter's morning to find that someone has shoved a tiny comet through your letterbox. Unwanted celestial light has faded the dado rail and a montage of family photographs is all askew from the eccentric orbit that it's assumed, on an axis from the umbrella stand to the cloakroom door.

Finding a comet in your junk mail is no easy thing to come to terms with. Imagine the frustration of wandering around Homebase, accosting blank-faced assistants to ask, 'Excuse me, do you sell humane traps for comets, by any chance?' Trying to discover which recycling bank to stuff a little comet into would be trickier than deciding what to do with bottles made from blue glass.

Then, finally, you'd probably just become resigned to its fascination for your hallway, even though its manners are worse than an untrained dog's. There it goes again, grubby and uncouth, leaping up and shedding stardust over unsuspecting guests.

Imagine the relief when it retreats to a den in the airing cupboard. What are a few ice-dampened blankets in the scheme of things? Compared to the inconvenience of swarms of amateur astronomers camped out on the staircase, recording meticulous observations from their vantage points and imperiously demanding copious quantities of strong, sweet tea.

Imagine, once again, that a comet has chosen to explore the confines of your house – don't make the easy mistake of thinking it's just a dirty snowball that some prankster has hurled through the letterbox. *This* is a real live comet, boldly going where no comet has ever gone before.

Freda Love Smith

Freda Love Smith is an American living in Nottingham. In the U.S. she played drums in rock bands such as The Blake Babies with Juliana Hatfield and The Mysteries of Life. Since relocating with her partner and children in 2006, she has turned her attention to writing fiction. She is a part-time student in Creative Writing at The University of Nottingham and is working on a novel.

Green Light

I was the only girl on the baseball team. You played piano in the school band, and had big green eyes, like double green lights.

We met at the mall to see *E.T.* with the little kid I was babysitting. He got scared, curled up on my lap, and I comforted him while you fed me popcorn. Once I almost choked and died from laughing while you stuffed a handful of popcorn into my mouth. We were a little pretend teen family, except happy. That night, trying to fall asleep, I whispered to myself, 'I think I have a boyfriend.' And what a boy.

Then you never called or took my calls again.

Ten years later in Iowa and still you had those eyes. I was galumphing down a steep, narrow staircase, my bass drum banging against my shins. Ninety-Nine percent of the time I loaded that drum out, some guy would 'little lady' me and offer to carry it or even just grab it out of my hands. But you squeezed right next to me, and I think admired my biceps. 'By the way,' you said, 'you should know – I date boys.' Had you rehearsed that line for years? *So what?* I thought. My drum scraped against the wall. I would have been your boy. Back then, we'd talk on the phone for three hours and it felt like five minutes. And you fed me popcorn. Who do you feed popcorn to now? I don't know about you, but that doesn't happen to me every day.

We got to the bottom of the stairs. You left arm-in-arm with your cute friends. I threw my drum in the van and smoked a cigarette on the curb.

The Bob Dylan Story

My dad tells me he beat this guy up at a party because he'd never heard of Bob Dylan. That's how strong his love was. He tells me love is always enough of a reason. It was 1966, the year before I was born, and my dad was a radical civil rights activist living in Nashville, Tennessee. There is a picture of him and my mother from that year, each holding acoustic guitars, smiling big smiles and gazing into each other's eyes. Playing Dylan songs, I'd guess. Did either of them think: I might hate you in five years?

The details of the beating-up incident are fuzzy. I wonder, what *was* his poison back then. And what is it now?

The thing I can't figure out is why I love this story so much, why it makes me happy. Why I can relate to it unquestioningly. It's not like I go around hitting people. I've never hit anyone.

The last time I went to a party, everybody there except me was an evangelical Christian. There were guitars, but no violence.

I work with this Welsh philosophy student. He told me he hates Bob Dylan. Thinks he's overrated. Listen, I said, my dad once punched a guy for not knowing Bob Dylan. If there's a gene for that, I've got it. So look out.

The Surrealist Manifesto

I used to rent an old woman's attic in Jamaica Plain, Massachusetts. There was no kitchen, just a kettle. I spent my time up there not eating, making strong cups of coffee, reading Andre Breton, reading Billy's letters, and writing letters to Billy. Come see me, I wrote.

He came. He saw my book on surrealism. You know what I want to read, he said. *The Surrealist Manifesto*. No, *I* said, I want to read *The Surrealist Manifesto*. Okay, we said. That settles what we're doing tomorrow.

Andre Breton believed in the magical properties of chance and coincidence.

I once read that a Scorpio and a Virgo would make an ideal detective team: we did. We discovered that the new bookstores were useless – *The Surrealist Manifesto* was out of print. The city library catalogue claimed there was a copy on the shelves but it had unaccountably disappeared. Someone was ahead of us. We visited one dusty bookshop after another, pausing in between only for coffee, cigarettes, and looking at each other.

Finally we were hungry and tired, but not tired of looking at each other. I suggested we eat something at the Museum School café, where I knew they quietly made the best sandwiches in town.

It was early Saturday evening; the school had emptied out. The glass-ceilinged atrium was full of tables piled with papers and Styrofoam cups. Chairs were scattered everywhere.

We bought sandwiches and set our trays on a messy table; right on top of a thick stack of paper.

My tray wobbled, so I lifted it up, uncovering:

The Surrealist Manifesto by Andre Breton.

A tidy, stapled, photocopy of the entire book.

We ate our sandwiches and talked about how amazing they were. I wondered, is this what the rest of my life will be like?

Casey Parry

Casey Parry loves lakes, mountains and the sea, but lives in a university town near the Fens. Casey's writings are disrupted by the family cats, hens and fish – and by an inability to stop being a student. Casey has been a member of CWIL (Cambridge Writers of Imaginative Literature) since it first began and finds the group a great outlet for her literal-minded pedantry and an immensely educational source of writerly feedback.

Hubris

The prince liked to emulate his heroes.

When he first saw the girl in the crystal casket, he was disappointed she wasn't guarded by brigades of basilisks or the odd gorgon. The dwarfs were merely an inconvenience, as they alternately haggled over the price of the coffin – their 'finest endeavour', 'worth a king's ransom' – or refused to part with their dead housekeeper.

Huntsmen manhandled the casket onto a wagon they'd liberated from some farm at the forest's edge. Then the prince dismissed his entire retinue. He had recently taken up the lyre. He alone would rescue his love from the darkest depths without once looking back. (He ordered the carter to do the same.)

He would do what Orpheus had not.

Behind the prince, the cart rattled along the forest track, jolting over stones and teetering precariously on the brink of huge potholes. The fragment of apple lodged in the girl's windpipe shook loose. She coughed, then attempted a breath.

The dwarfs had been correct: their craftsmanship was the finest. The casket was solidly constructed with no flaw to impede a clear view of its contents, no means of admitting corruption from outside.

The girl's eyes flew open as she discovered her predicament. She pushed against the lid with all her strength, scrabbled at the smooth interior searching for some means of escape. She shouted at the rustic sat up front on the cart. And to the man on horseback. And to the crowds that had gathered at the forest's edge. Not a whisper reached them.

As he rode on, the prince barely noticed the peasants who lined the way. He ignored their ill-mannered shouts and gestures at his beauteous prize.

He stared straight ahead contemplating fame.

Rich Hough

Rich is a writer who trained as a scientist at Oxford University. His introduction to ecology, *You Can Save the Planet* (originally published by A&C Black), has been translated into German, Spanish and Catalan. His short stories have appeared in *Pen Pusher Magazine* and in Leaf Books' 2007 Micro-Fiction anthology, *Imagine Coal and More Micro-Fiction*. Rich wrote and directed *NightSchool*, a series of comedy shows for The Theatre Museum, Covent Garden; and is co-writing a new, darker comedy for Radio 4, *The Chiller Cabinet*. Against all odds, he still lives with a wonderful man in North London.

Causality Doesn't Work Like That

A man met another man on Turnpike Lane, in a bar called Catch 22, and they got talking.

The second man said to the first, 'I know you, don't I?'

And the first man replied, 'I don't think so.'

And the second man said, 'Well, I might not know you now, but I will do tomorrow.'

The first man giggled because he thought the second man was just being coy, but here's the thing: he wasn't.

The second man explained, 'I'm a Time Traveller. My yesterdays are your tomorrow. We're going to meet for the first time, my time, outside your house on Turnpike Lane, tomorrow afternoon at five o'clock.'

'Golly,' said the first man. 'In that case, what are tomorrow night's lottery numbers?'

And the second man said, '14, 16, 21, 30, 39 and 42.'

The next day, a man left his house in Turnpike Lane to buy a lottery ticket. He had the form already filled out but, being a clumsy son-of-a-gun, he dropped it on the pavement. A second man picked it up and handed it back to him.

The first man said to the second, 'You know me, don't you?'

And the second man replied, 'I don't think so.'

And the first man said, 'Well, you might not know me now, but you will do tomorrow. You're a Time Traveller. My tomorrows are your yesterday. Last time we met, my time, you gave me these lottery numbers.' And he held up the form and the second man read:

'14, 16, 21, 30, 39 and 42. *I must try to remember.*'

Later that evening, the winning lottery numbers were announced as 3, 8, 12, 26, 28 and 40, not 14, 16, 21, 30, 39 and 42 because causality doesn't work like that.

Margaretta Jones

Margaretta Jones, a retired teacher, lives in Kent in close proximity to her children and grandchildren. This is a constant source of joy to both her husband and herself. She is a short story writer who has recently become attracted – almost addicted – to mini-fiction. Its discipline is a challenge, which she relishes. She has had short stories published in various anthologies and small press magazines including *Cambrensis, Granary Writers, Writers' Express* and *Senior Moments*. One of her short stories was short-listed and read on Radio Kent. She writes for pleasure and is a member of two writing circles where she meets and enjoys the company of like-minded people. At present she attends a creative writing course at Ashford WEA.

A Day in the Country

They sat under a canopy of bougainvillea entwined with jasmine. The heady perfume, in addition to the torrid heat, brought on her migraine.

'I can't eat much,' she said, taking a sip of sweet white Muscat wine. She would rather they had a carafe of water but this was a special visit to Picasso's favourite haunt and she didn't wish to appear petty.

He toyed with a bowl of salade niçoise, mopping up the juice with chunks of local bread. His lips glistened with a mixture of olive oil and garlic. She dipped a napkin into her glass, reached over and slicked them clean.

'The wine's good,' he said. 'Let's have another glass – but you must eat something.' She peeled a tangerine and sucked the juice from each segment; squashed a purple plum until it felt mushy then shared the flesh with him.

'We'll have a coffee later,' she said. 'It'll be cooler then and maybe I shall manage a little Mousse au Chocolat.'

He took her into the house, which smelt of thyme and lemons. Grabbing a couple from a blue bowl, he threw one into the air but it dropped onto the cobbled floor and split open. The old woman in black sitting near the door glowered her disapproval.

He stood like a statue, mesmerized by Picasso's skill, his brush strokes painted directly onto the stone walls. A genius or a sham, she wondered, but said nothing. He was lost in admiration at the originality of the artist.

'One day I shall paint you,' he said, engrossed in the woman minus a nose, an eye in place of a navel, her skin a mess of green and purple blotches, a wisp of hair creeping into an ear.

She remained silent.

But he became a plastic surgeon striving for perfection; she was long forgotten.

A Precious Possession

I'm no better than anyone. Worse than most in his eyes.

I can laugh now but it wasn't funny at the time. There I was, head held high, wheeling Flora, my new baby in her 'Silver Cross' pram with the chocolate brown hood, down Princes Street in the direction of the shops.

I'd lived in ballooning clothes for so long it was time for a treat. I dropped a bag of maternity outfits into Oxfam then walked towards Monsoon. And you'll never guess – I forgot all about Flora. Imagine that! My own flesh and blood discarded like an old glove. And to make matters worse, when I finished browsing, I took the bus home.

Of course, Alistair was livid.

'People like you get committed every day,' he said.

Did I feel the most neglectful mother in the whole world? Alistair insisted on driving down to pick her up, forgetting that the expensive pram I had saved for over the months was there too.

When I challenged him he retorted, 'You can't equate an accessory like a pram to a baby,' and that was the end of the conversation.

So I find myself walking down the same street early next morning. Alistair was working at home and insisted on doing everything for Flora as though I were now totally incapable.

I returned triumphantly, pushing my gorgeous pram, gave it a gentle polish and left it standing in the hall.

The next morning it had gone.

'You're not fit to be in charge of it,' he said. 'Look, I've bought a sling instead. You can't possibly forget Flora if she's practically attached to you.'

So there was Flora clinging to me like a limpet and my beautiful pram gone forever.

Some things are really too painful to forgive.

Lorraine Cave

Lorraine Cave grew up in West London and has worked in a number of diverse places such as a hotel in Scotland, Kew Gardens and Jersey Zoo. She's mother to two wonderful daughters. She began writing in 2006, following advice given in the *Daily Telegraph*'s Novel in a Year column which inspired her to sign up for a Start Writing Fiction course with the Open University. The Leaf Books publication *Imagine Coal and More Micro-Fiction* contained three of her pieces. Lorraine is a part-time pet-sitter/dog walker and lives with her partner in the beautiful county of Cornwall.

What Stinks

'Can you smell something?' she asks, sitting up in bed. It's 3.30am for God's sake and I want to shout *Shut up!* – but I know better than that.

'No. I can't smell anything,' I mumble into my pillow.

'Are you sure? It's really strong.'

'Okay. What does it smell like?' I bet she says 'fumes'.

'It's like smoked haddock.' *Well, that's a bit different.* 'Wait a minute.' There are several loud sniffs. 'Maybe it's gas. No, it's more like fumes. Definitely fumes.' *Bingo!*

I tell you, the woman is paranoid. And what's worse, I live with her twenty-four hours a day. It's driving me totally insane but time has taught me one thing; it's taught me to gauge my responses so that she doesn't have a panic attack. Because Tracey's panic attacks are well worth avoiding.

'Are you sure you can't smell it? It's like exhaust fumes.' If she doesn't shut up I'll tell her what *really* stinks. Doing time: that's what stinks. Doing time for slipping a knife between the ribs of an abusive, psychotic bastard. It turned out he wasn't heartless after all.

I don't know what *she* did to get herself in here but I'll tell you one thing: her kids never visit. Maybe they can't, if you know what I mean.

'There's no fumes, no gas and most definitely no haddock. Go to sleep, Tracey,' I say in a calm monotone. Soon she'll be snoring while I lie awake thinking about the two blond-haired boys in the photo that she keeps hidden in her drawer.

I wonder if remorse has a smell? It's one of those 3.30 in the morning questions. If it does then I'll be the last to know.

Rosie Garland

Born in London to a runaway teenager, Rosie Garland has always been a cuckoo in the nest. She has three solo collections of poems, widely anthologised short stories and has been featured in *Mslexia* and *Succour* magazines. Her first novel, *Animal Instinct*, is with her agent. She has an eclectic writing and performance history, from 80s Goth band The March Violets, to twisted cabaret as alter ego 'Rosie Lugosi the Vampire Queen'. She has won the DaDa Award for Performance Artist of the Year, the Diva Award for Solo Performer, and a Poetry Award from the People's Café, New York.

www.myspace.com/rosiegarland
www.myspace.com/rosielugosi

Sadie Jones Took Me Line-Dancing

Sadie Jones is a cowgirl. She's my mum's new friend, but isn't like a mother. She's got this thing she does with her eyes: you know she's never changed a nappy.

My mum has taken up dancing. It's one of her new pursuits since Dad's affair with Brian really worked out.

'It's not to meet men,' she tells me. 'Or women,' she adds, like I'd be worried about that.

She met Sadie at Tap; they moved onto Latin: now it's fringed shirts and boots with Cuban heels. Sadie laughs a lot. It makes mum laugh too, and that's got to be an improvement.

Dancing's not my thing; but it's hard to say no to Sadie. She holds her mouth just so, as if she's saying *you want to have fun, too?* without speaking any words. It's not like I haven't had girlfriends. It's just that with Sadie's mouth and eyes put together, I'm not interested in anyone else.

Sadie says, 'I've got a spare shirt'll fit you'.

I say, 'S'pose'.

She says, 'And a western tie'.

I say, 'S'pose'.

Mum tells me to stop being so miserable; they're going and I'm coming too.

I say, 'S'pose'.

I hold Sadie's hand in the bit where we pair up and go round in a circle, lay my palm on the curve of her back. She tells me I look hot.

On the way home Mum says, 'Well, you enjoyed yourself, didn't you? After all that moaning?'

I say, 'S'pose'.

Heirloom Quality

I don't go for older women; the old-enough-to-be-your-mother type. So it was a surprise to everyone. She was a lecturer in Gender Studies, and I'm studying Law, so it wasn't like I was in her class. She went for me as much as I went for her. We were adults; it was equal. My grades did not suffer.

I'd gone round to her place (she was hardly coming round to my dump). We ate. I opened a bottle of red from the wine rack; poured most of it for her. Watched her shoulders loosen. By the time we got off the sofa and headed up the stairs she was as slack-limbed as a fresher. I grabbed the hair at the back of her neck and she fell onto my mouth.

When we'd finished it was too early to sleep and too late for me to go: the night buses were rubbish and she didn't offer to help out with a cab. She knitted her fingers on top of the duvet.

'What's up?' I asked, wondering if we'd been found out by the Dean.

'I've got something I want to show you,' she said.

She wobbled to the dressing table and tugged at the bottom drawer; bent over and brought out a baby, cradling it in her arms.

'She's mid-Victorian,' she cooed. 'Incredibly rare in this kind of condition. The christening gown's Edwardian. This is Elizabeth.'

The room bulged with the smell of camphor.

'Real hair,' she murmured, smoothing the sleek waves. 'The very best. Eastern European for this colour and quality. Aren't you, darling?'

It took me a second to register she was talking to the doll. I decided not to tell her my grandmother was a Polish Jew. The porcelain eyes clicked open and shut. I didn't make a fuss. I left after breakfast. My grades did not suffer.

Maureen Gallagher

Maureen Gallagher is a retired resource teacher living in Galway. She started writing poetry and fiction in 1998 and since then has had her work published in literary magazines worldwide and broadcast on RTE. She's been shortlisted for awards many times and won first prize in the Wicklow Writers' poetry competition 2008 and second in the short story category. She was also shortlisted in 2008 for the Tigh Neactain Sonnet Competition, the Chuairt bilingual poetry competition, the Trim satire competition and was commended for Leaf Books' short story competition.

An African Plant Begins with an O

The alert. Coming up to the roundabout. Suddenly – where is she going? Oh Jesus! Where? Where, which exit? WHICH EXIT! City Centre? Clifden? Dublin? Where is she going? City Centre? Clifden? Dublin? THE DENTIST! Third exit. Oh, thank God! Whew!

Crosswords are useful. And she sets herself little tasks now on her daily walk. Like today. Memorising the names of the estates – Rosan Glas, Ceide House, Rosleic. The liquid feel of the words on her tongue. She loves words. And look! That flower again. Idling like an exotic visitor in someone's garden. South African. Quite different from the South African house plant she used grow on her kitchen sill. But that was aons ago. Before she left home to find herself. It was called *African* somethingorother, oh Jesus, African … African … VIOLET! African violet! Got it!

Now this one. Shape like a daisy. A big fat daisy. A great favourite, although it'd take over a whole garden if you didn't watch. Pale narrow petals. What's this it's called? Something beginning with O. Osymanthus? Something like osymanthus. A name you could chew. Mesembryanthemum? No! It has to begin with O. God, she thought she had it for a minute there. Mesembryanthemum: a daisy too and South African. At least she had the genus right. Close. But not there.

Nearly home. Osy … osy … oste … … oste … ostesper … … OSTEOSPERSUM! THAT'S IT! Ten out of ten! Osteospersum! What a gift! Osteospersum!

Helen Pizzey

Helen Pizzey holds an MA in Creative Writing from Bath Spa University College. She has had poems published in several UK anthologies and magazines, including *Mslexia* and *The Interpreter's House*, as well as in *The Orange Coast Review* in America. Another of her poems has just been set for a large-scale choral and orchestral work commissioned under the Per Cent for Art Scheme in Ireland. Her short-fiction appears in two anthologies previously published by Leaf Books.

Invisibility for Beginners

First, remove all colour from your wardrobe – especially white; white is eye-catching and stands out in a crowd. Cultivate a monotone and low velocity speech, talking only about yourself. Try to sound unenthusiastic. Your effectiveness can be monitored by cornering someone at a party, a safe distance from the kitchen, bathroom and drinks, making sure they already have a full glass in their hand: if their eyes glaze over, nostrils start to flare and their jaw sets in suppression of a yawn, you will know you are getting the hang of at least fading into the wallpaper.

Next, try sitting in a disused shop doorway along with discarded fast-food containers and jettisoned junk mail. A reduced sensitivity to smell is necessary to complete this stage successfully. Don't be tempted to draw attention to yourself by urinating in the corner. Further develop your skill by donning a colourful fund-raising T-shirt and pamphleteering homeward-bound commuters heading for the tubes: this really tests your increased personal invisibility range once you have mastered the basics.

On no account stand on draughty street corners sandwiched between boards proclaiming The End Is Nigh. This has been known to result in personal eradication or even, in extreme circumstances, sudden death and is only to be attempted by those who have previously attained Level 3 Disappearance.

Good luck with the training. I look forward to not seeing you soon.

Andrea Davies

Andrea Davies is from Liverpool. She specialises in Equality and Diversity and has worked for a number of major organisations. She owes her love of reading and writing to her amazing mum who taught her to read and write at the age of three. She has been writing most of her life, but has always filed her work in the bin. Her wonderful husband Colin has finally persuaded her to stop binning her work and to take a sabbatical to pursue her dream of writing for a living. The Leaf Micro-Fiction competition is the first she has entered.

Beside the Seaside

She sat heavily on the pebbles, her shopping trolley a windbreak by her side. The seagulls mourned on her behalf. Had she been of another culture, another place, she could have screeched along with them, tearing her clothes, wailing, weeping, manifesting her grief.

She had thrown his ashes in the waves and could hear his breathing now, in and out, in and out, as the waves carried him towards her, surging up the beach, closer, closer. She picked up one of the bigger pebbles – or cobbles as he would have corrected her. She felt him, his skin, his bones, warm in her hand, in the stone.

Gavin Eyers

Gavin Eyers is in his last minute twenties and lives contentedly in Greenwich, South-East London. He works in a post room where he delivers words to others all morning then goes home to write his own. Gavin is mid-way through a degree in Literature and immersed in the wonderful stress of writing his first novel. When not writing he can usually be found wrecking his body in the gym or nurturing it in the pub. This is his first published story.

Light

He would drunkenly run around our bed-sit with his hands pressed together, winding them from side to side, imitating the guppies. I'd laugh so hard I couldn't draw a breath. We were eighteen then.

Babies began to arrive, one then another. One each year at the start of our twenties. Days out came too, as did visits and kisses from aunties, gasps from delighted grandparents.

Now we get visits and doting attention from children and grandchildren. We behave sensibly, as you should, y'know.

When they've gone home he presses his hands together, swims around the room.

Jon Prawer

Behold

Behold, I am Grammoth. I have brought forth generations, and the generations have brought forth generations. Worlds are overrun with my spawn, and otherworlds. Consuming fires have been lit in my name, and great empires toppled. My sons have looked upon the barren waste of continents, their sons have seen whole worlds destroyed, and theirs defiled the vastnesses of space.

Look, Nan's dropped off.

She's catching flies.

Let's balance a spoon on her nose.

Douglas Bruton

Douglas Bruton is a teacher at a high school near Edinburgh in Scotland. He graduated from the University of Aberdeen with honours in English and Philosophy. But it was later, at Edinburgh College of Art, that he discovered he could write. He has been writing ever since. He has gained recognition in over forty UK based writing competitions over the past two years, and in one or two across the water in America. He has also been published in many competition anthologies as well as in *The Eildon Tree Literary Magazine, Transmission,* and *Cadenza.*

A Pebble from the River for Annie

Annie in the shadows, a shadow herself, shoes off, creeping barefoot through the moon-radiant street, to the church with its windows blank and its door shut fast. And Annie, with a babe cradled in her arms, and her small fist making little noise on the locked door.

Annie cross with the minister, cross with god, cross with all men, kneeling in the dew-damp grass at the river's edge. She must have a name for the child she delivered herself in the gagged dark of the barn; she knew what to do, had seen lambs Spring-born to ewes. Annie cupping her hand, scooping water from the river, and wetting the baby's head, as she'd watched the minister do at the stone font in the church, and calling her Judith.

Annie at the river, her night-black hair like a veil, muttering prayers and songs never heard in any church. And the moon in the sky, and a pebble from the river for Annie.

Annie back through the village, seeing the bakehouse lit up like the sun slept there, the ovens already hot and the smell of new bread leaking out to where Annie is. The door open and a man singing, and his wife laughing somewhere in the back. Annie, then, kissing her child and laying her down inside the door where it's warm.

At the far reach of the village Annie finding her shoes where she left them, putting a pebble in one, hard and round, and ever after limping as she goes – not that she needed a stone to remind her of what she had done. And Judith growing through the quickening years, singing in church like her father, and laughing like her mother; but not like Annie, except that her hair was dark, glossy-black like the wings of crows.

Mary Pooley

Mary Pooley lives in Reading and is a member of the Thames Valley Writers' Circle. She is a retired housewife whose husband now does most of her work. Her hobbies are grandchildren, reading and writing. She gave up trying to get an 'O level' in English Language after failing the exam on three occasions. Until a couple of years ago, most of her writing was poetry, but now she has started writing very short stories, some of which are more like glimpses into her characters' lives.

Movin' On

If you wanna meet a loser, shake my hand.

Man, if you were to stand at the bottom of my family tree you wouldn't see one leaf, not one single leaf. It's all bare wood up there.

The dead don't matter much, but some of us are still alive. Alive and kickin' our heels. Bangin' our heads against closed doors.

I might've been born in the gutter but now I'm movin' on.

Gonna start a new family tree and I'll be right at the top. And when I die, I'll look up from my grave and watch the buds growin'. I'll see the blossom hangin' down above my head and there'll be leaves to shade me from the burnin' sun. There'll be fruit so heavy it'll test the strength of every branch. And the taste, man, it'll taste as sweet as suckin' sugar cane.

How am I gonna do it? I'm gonna write a book. The story of my life. I'm gonna dish up everythin' I can remember. But I ain't gonna say what I did, or what I thought, or what I said. No way. I'm gonna write what I should've done, what I should've thought, what I should've said.

And when I finish the book, I'm gonna sit right down and read about this new man I've become. Then all the feelings that I used to have will shrivel up and die. Jus' like my old family tree.

Then I'll stand in the middle of the crossroads, with this book in my hand, and whichever road I take will be the right one.

Andrea Tang

Andrea Tang is Malaysian by birth, Chinese by ethnicity and British by nationality. She graduated in the summer of 2008 from the University of Huddersfield with a BA(Hons) English Language with Creative Writing degree, and is due to begin a MA Modern English Language course at the same university in the autumn. Her poem 'Lost' has been short-listed in the Spring 2008 Earlyworks Press Open Poetry Competition and is to appear in an anthology later in the year. Andrea lives in Huddersfield with her parents and elder sister, constantly juggling between study, creative writing and martial arts practice (being a black belt in 'Tang Soo Do').

Weather Goddess

Old lethargy hangs off the stranger like torn threads of dangling spider webbing. He verbally unloads his heavy thoughts into your reluctant ears.

'During a January week, my weather goddess was experiencing another spell of bad moods and chucking down hail at me. You know, when her thunderous temperament stains the floor a dismal colour, like tombstone grey paint spilt over a canvas; when she lashes out with gale force words, rattling windows as if soaked tramps were banging on them; when her torrential tears batter the ground, a merciless bombardment of H_2O bullets that make you keep your head down and dive for the nearest cover.

You know the emotionally unstable weather I'm speaking about. All married men have invoked the turbulence of a weather goddess. You'd think a man with any sense would snuggle up by the fire indoors on his own with a blanket around his shoulders, cupping a mug of hot tea. He'd be feeling grateful to have a roof over his head protecting him from the moody wrath of a weather goddess.

She determines the weather in every man's life. She's a divine being that comes in various pleasing forms. But her unpredictable emotional hurricanes demand reverence and appeasement, or sometimes you just have to wait for her storm to pass. When she snows, you can guess she's probably giving you the cold treatment. When you feel her gentle breezes, she'll be feeling touchy and want to stroke you. A goddess's elemental moods fluctuate as plentifully and speedily as chameleon skin colours. Please her and she will radiate summer rays to warm your life; displease her and her icicled heart will summon arctic frost.'

He shakes his head wearily.

You sigh and say, 'Better wrap up warm for the winter then'.

Christine Genovese

Christine Genovese has been an avid reader from earliest childhood. She developed a passion for literature and language, which she channelled into a teaching career and an ongoing sideline in writing. She's an eclectic writer (and reader) and enjoys experimenting with a variety of genres and disciplines. Some of her short stories have appeared in small press magazines and she has also had a number of articles published on subjects as diverse as dogs, spinning and auxiliary verbs. Christine has been living in rural Normandy for the last sixteen years.

Victor

The taxidermist's rimless glasses sparkled with pride when he showed me into his workshop to view Victor. I came close to letting out a roar of protest. Instead I managed a stiff polite smile and tried to make the right noises while writing out the cheque.

It could easily have paid for the holiday Gary and I should have had together.

On the way home in the car I let rip. I howled like a hurt animal and tears of frustration and failure flowed freely down my face. Victor had let me down – giving out the wrong message.

A stuffed animal ('We don't stuff animals. We sculpture the body in polyurethane foam and fit the cured skin over it', the taxidermist had corrected me). Nevertheless, a 'stuffed' animal is supposed to be hideously grotesque, isn't it? Its pathetic attempt at remaining in your life ought to yell at you for having abandoned it.

Not Victor. He stood there, as proud and unapproachable as ever, dewlap extended and dorsal crest erect. A green iguana nearly six feet long who'd shared my house for the last two years. As had Gary. Next he'd start head-bobbing to warn me I was an unwelcome intruder.

'You just haven't got the touch,' Gary would say, kneeling down to caress Victor. I watched Victor's eyes close as his head nudged into Gary's gentle hand.

Victor had let himself die when Gary left. ('Sixteen years. Not a bad age for a green iguana,' the vet said.) I should have asked the taxidermist to stuff him (okay: *preserve* him) lying on his back, stumpy legs in the air and eyes closed. That would have given out the right message.

I could feel the polyurethane foam slowly hardening inside me.

Robert Lankamp

Like many other writers, Robert Lankamp dabbled in various genres – notably punk poetry and black humour science fiction – before he finally settled on writing about the funny aliens next door. He lives near the beach with his dog (Jimmy) in the pleasant seaside city of The Hague, Holland. You'll be relieved to hear that he has finally achieved a thin veneer of respectability as an English professor at Leiden.

They Say that Belgium is a Nice Country

The hotel bar was as quiet as a dream.

'You want to share a bottle of wine?' I asked.

'You still drink wine by the bottle?'

I ordered a glass of Merlot. You wanted a Chablis.

'We'll get back together,' I said. 'We'll have a baby.'

I drank my Merlot, while you stared at your Chablis, and then finally took a tiny sip.

'Can I hold your hand?' I asked.

'Sure, go ahead.'

Your hand felt like a dead bird.

'A baby,' you said. 'My hope always was that you'd have donated sperm and that you'd die early enough for me to have the baby.'

I let go of your hand, and you used it to reach into your bag for bottles of pills that you shook out onto a napkin.

'I'm emotionally lost,' you said. 'First I tried Amsterdam with you, and then for ten years I tried the American dream with Charlie. Now not only does he want the house, but he wants the cat, and the dog. Then I found out that my stepfather broke my arm when I was two. My psychiatrist says I have post-traumatic stress syndrome.'

'Maybe it's not so bad to be lost for a little while.' I gently squeezed your arm.

'Ouch!' You filled your hand with pills. 'Can I have some water?' you asked the bartender.

'We'll have a baby,' I tried again.

You tapped your finger against your wine glass. 'All I want is a baby. They say that Belgium is a nice country.'

'We'll make a baby. And then we'll see. All right?' I wanted to take hold of your hand again, but you'd grasped the stem of your glass as if you hoped it'd keep you from disappearing.

Keith Souter

Keith Souter is a part time family doctor, newspaper columnist and novelist. He is married with three grown-up children and lives within arrow-shot of Sandal Castle, the scene of his latest historical novel, *The Pardoner's Crime*. He has published nine medical books, several of which been translated into six languages, and nine novels in three genres. He is a member of the Crime Writers Association and of International Thriller Writers. He enjoys the challenge of micro-fiction and has previously won a couple of short fiction prizes, including the 2006 Fish One-Page Historical Prize. Apart from writing, he enjoys good books, fine wine, cinema and golf.

Satisfaction

'I demand satisfaction! Choose your weapons.'

My head snapped backwards and I felt blood trickle down my chin.

'You shall have it,' said I, dabbing my cut lip. 'Pistols! When and where would you like to die?'

Mon dieu! The satisfaction on his part was going to be as short lived as his life. All right, so I may have sullied the Tussaud wench's honour, but she should have been honoured to be dishonoured by one such as I.

'At dawn,' he replied insolently. 'Above Paris.'

Ha! The fool desires death. Not only am I a crack shot; I am also the greatest balloonist in France. And who is he? Somebody Montgolfier? The runt of a once proud ballooning family. It will give me satisfaction to crush their name in the dust of history.

It was misty at dawn when my balloon rose majestically and I sailed above the city, peering through the vapours. I found him waiting above Notre Dame, in the basket beneath a dingy grey balloon. He was poised, duelling fashion, his pistol cocked and aimed, yet he did not fire.

Pah! I despise honourable fools. I blew the top off his head and watched as he slumped backwards into the basket. Then I reloaded and shot a hole in his balloon and laughed as it quickly deflated and spiralled earthwards.

I was still watching when I saw the muzzle-flash from below, then heard the tearing of the envelope above me.

Now as I fall from the sky I see Montgolfier and the Tussaud wench atop Notre Dame. He has a musket in his hands and she is showering him with kisses. I grudgingly salute them as I go to my inglorious end, duped by their mannequin.

The Devil take them and their satisfaction.

Lloyd Markham

Lloyd Alexander Markham was born in South Africa in 1988. He grew up in Zimbabwe and moved to Wales along with his mother, father and older sister in 2004. He is currently residing in Bridgend and is doing a degree in Creative & Professional Writing at the University of Glamorgan where he is about to begin his second year.

The Factory for Other People's Happiness

Hello. My name is John and I work in a factory that produces a most unusual commodity. Happiness. Other people's, to be precise. Most things produced in factories are made for the express purpose of making at least someone happy, but, that being said, the factory I work in is rather different.

Other manufacturing facilities produce commodities that merely make people happy; the factory I work in produces actual raw happiness itself. We do it by essentially crushing – milking, if you will – the happiness out of everyday objects. You'll be surprised how much of it you can find in a fruit, a teddy bear, or even a book. The source of happiness we use is old family photographs as they're potent and relatively cheap to acquire. Specialists get the photos from the homes of deceased widows and a conveyer belt feeds the photos into the Machine.

I'm not quite sure what the technical name for the Machine is, actually, or how it works or who made it. All I really know is that photos go in and happiness comes out. Of course we never actually see the happiness we make as it's pumped to a different part of the factory.

It's occurred to me that I use the word 'we' a lot, which is problematic as I'm not quite sure who 'we' are. You see, the daytime staff consists of one person. Me. All the actual production is done by the Machine and my job is simply making sure the Machine does its job, so for the most part I'm alone during my shift. Apparently some guy works evenings, but I've never met him. I'm not even sure what sort of people buy our product. All I know is I certainly can't afford it.

Laura Tansley

Laura Tansley is from Malvern in Worcestershire, which she credits as a place of inspiration but only when she is distanced from it. This led her to Glasgow where she is now studying for her PhD in English Literature. She is previously unpublished and encouraged by the commendations received from Leaf.

Field

Her sandals scooped up dry ground, depositing leaves and stones under the bridge of her feet. Every so often she would step down awkwardly, pause, lean against a tree and empty her shoes. Her escort would've noticed she was gone by now, but she had already walked a mile. By the time she'd smoked and got back again, he wouldn't have left the army base.

Summer in Yugoslavia had dried out the fields to a dull sandy colour that at dusk had flushed ochre. She stood in one of these fields and lit the joint with a match, letting the smell of sulphur sting and the smoke massage her. Her brain was weary of thinking and speaking in a handful of languages. She wanted to feel obliterated. Her mother had decided that the conflict between unknowable men was more desirable than the turmoil of divorce so together they talked incessantly and dreamt in several tongues.

Whilst re-lighting, she noticed the mines. The ground was so perfectly undisturbed. Cylindrical mounds innocently arranged. Squatting down like a coiling spring she sought the safe path that had led her to this disembodying present but her dulled mind could not find it.

A man walked passed shouting in Serbian, 'Mine field'. She replied, 'I fucking know', in English. He wouldn't understand. There was little he could do.

It became dark. She would have to wait until dawn, about six hours away. It wasn't cold – she was thankful for that – but she held her legs tightly. She imagined body parts being pulled from her, but she couldn't imagine the pain. That remained illusively surreal.

The lifting of the morning mist let her slip with the sand back through the hourglass till she was sat on top of the perfect dune of now. She pointed and flexed her fingers.

We are all the Same Person in the Crowd, for an Instant

The bite mark inside my cheek sweats and boasts as my tongue rolls over it like a pawing kitten. I can't leave it alone. The lift doors open with the sound of a yawn and I step out. I catch a look into the faces of the people about to step into my practical joke but I don't laugh. This is not because it's not funny.

I have been doing this for a while: pressing the button for my floor, then the eleven other buttons so that whoever gets in after me (maybe they're going to the special collections on twelve, escorted by an employee of the library with gloves and a cloth to wipe the breath marks from glass cases, or to the map room where endless drawings of the beige Earth are filed by country of origin) will visit every subject.

When I leave for the Summer to rest and travel and rest again, I leave the faces that I think I will remember but never do. When I return, there are posters stuck inside the lifts asking, '*Please* do not press the buttons for all of the floors. This causes unnecessary wear and tear to the cables and creates congestion'. The thought of unravelling twine makes me take my cheek between my teeth again and I am sad to realise that the queues of unsuspecting accomplices in my game must not have remembered my face either and forgotten their reasons for retaliating.

William Letford

William Letford lives in Stirling and works as a roofer. This year he has been published in *New Writing Scotland* and *Poetry Scotland*. He has been accepted into the Mlitt in Creative Writing at Glasgow University and received a New Writer's Award from the Scottish Book Trust.

Where There's Smoke

My father is sitting on the centre cushion of the sofa. His legs are crossed at the ankles and his arms are folded over his chest. He's watching *The Bill*. I'm not watching television. I'm on the armchair with a bowl of cornflakes in front of me. I'm holding the bowl with my left hand and spooning the flakes into my mouth with my right hand.

'Donald,' my mother shouts from the kitchen. 'Donald, you've left the grill on again. Every time. Every time you cook you leave the grill on. You're going to burn the fucking house down.'

My father doesn't react. He keeps his legs crossed at the ankles and his arms folded over his chest. He watches *The Bill*. I finish my cornflakes. The spoon clinks against the bowl as I scoop the last of the milk into my mouth. I get up. I pass my mother as she leaves the kitchen and enters the living room. She doesn't look at me but she speaks to me as she walks by.

'He'll burn the fucking house down so he will and good fucking luck to him.' She's carrying a bowl of tomato soup.

I walk into the kitchen and open the door of the dishwasher. The dishwasher is full of clean dishes. I leave the bowl in the sink and notice that my mother has left the hob on. The circle of blue flame holds my attention for a moment. I turn off the gas then I walk out of the kitchen and through the living room to look at the front door. I can see the key. It's in the lock. In case of fire, they'll escape quickly.

Stewart Tiley

Born and raised in Somerset, Stewart Tiley has subsequently lived in Lancashire, Yorkshire, Hertfordshire, Bedfordshire and Cambridgeshire, studying in Lancaster, Leeds and Manchester. He currently lives just outside Cambridge, where he is librarian at Sidney Sussex College (the one with Cromwell's head). Several years ago he was a runner up in another writing competition. That's about it really.

Infested

I had some shoes once, but they got infested. So dad had to get rid of them. He put on the rubber gloves and lit the bonfire. I sat on the cold stone bench and picked the seeds out of my veruccas with a pin. Mum brought me some plasters and some clean socks. She patted my head and said, 'Don't worry, lover, it won't always be this way.' She was wrong.

I liked those shoes. We bought them specially for Maggie and Ray's wedding. They had a badge, all metal and shiny, come with them. I wore it to school and showed Miss Higson. She was very impressed. We all went down the shop to get them: me, Mum, Dad, Becca, Nanna Cumbershall, and Uncle Keith. I chose them cos they had good grips, and they were lace ups. Everyone thought they were good. Mum and Becca went off to look at ladies' shoes. The assistant got the foot-gauge out, and Nanna tutted cos my socks were hanging off. She pulled them up but then my toes peeked through the end. Nanna raised her eyes to high heaven. I went and sat down so the assistant could measure me. She bent over my foot as she slid the block down, her hair and blouse hanging loose. Suddenly Dad and Uncle Keith came and sat either side of me. It was all tickly and nice, especially when she tightened the tape to check the width. 'He's a 12F,' she said to my Dad, who gave a little start, as though his mind had been on other things. And then, just when it couldn't get any better, she did the other one. That was my favourite day, better than all the others, before everything got infested.

Amy Mackelden

Amy Mackelden studied Creative Writing at Cardiff, currently lives in Newcastle Upon Tyne, and one day hopes to move to New York. The Isle of Wight will always be where she is from, and micro-fiction, her drug of choice.

The Eskimo Word(s) for Love

We cut through the snow to make an igloo, get inside it like kids, your face giving you away before your voice does, and my hands, hypothermic, touching your skin but not feeling anything. It takes hours until the tips of my fingers are pink again and longer before they don't sting.

Sometimes, I catch your eye, in between snow drifts. We change our shoes without breaking stares. I think about proposing this way. That, or in an igloo, hands fumbling in my pocket for a square box that I can't properly grip, and which I drop before I manage to open. The words don't make it out of my mouth before your eyes, consistently blue in spite of lighting, say 'yes.' Later, I try again properly, my hands in your mittens at your house, clumsily flipping the lip of the ring box with a thumb and clumped-together fingers. Then, you completely see what you are to me – sparkly and silver and totally irreplaceable.

I will savour you until there's nothing left – until your back gives out whilst shoveling snow and your hands can't recover from frostbite. I'll tie your laces before tying mine up. And if I don't die first, I will pass you on like an heirloom. Make it obvious you're worth more than the will makes out. Or I'll bury you where our hearts sparked, knee deep in an igloo, where one day you'll be another crisp discovery in snow.

Sara Benham

Sara Benham lives in Somerset with her partner and two children. She writes as a community correspondent for Mid Somerset Newspapers and also works part time as an estate agent. Sara began writing short stories and comedy sketches after attending a year-long creative writing course at her local college. Humour plays a big part in Sara's writing and in her life: she also writes and performs stand up comedy. Sara was a semi-finalist in the 2008 Nivea Funny Women awards, and her comedy sketch 'The Dog' was included in the BAFTA winning *Blowout* sketch show on Channel 4.

Whiskey and Cigarettes

Mr Hill at the store told me I was sassy today, like a foaming can of sarsaparilla. I knew what he meant, and he didn't mean sassy at all. I've seen him looking at me different since I got my hair all golden and got myself a cute little skirt. But I ain't interested. Now I've turned twenty-one I can go to Jimmy's bar, and there's nothing Pa can do about it.

Devlin drinks at Jimmy's. I've watched him going in there before supper. Course, Devlin ain't his real name. I have no true idea as to what his real name might be, but Susanna reckons he looks like he's got the Devil in him, so Devlin it is.

I'm already there, at the bar when Devlin comes in. He don't notice me at first. I see the way the other guys look; like I'm about to give them the finest fried chicken and mashed potatoes they ever had in their entire lives. Devlin sees me, and he's as hungry as the rest of them.

I place a filter tip between my lips, and slide off the stool. He looks at me so deeply, I fear he may truly be the devil himself and he's tugging at my very soul. I smile, and the cigarette falls from my mouth. He don't take his eyes off me. He picks it up, running it between his fingers.

It feels like a million Jackhammers are stamping on my heart. I turn to my whiskey. The ice is almost melted away.

The bar's getting crowded and he's next to me now, so close I can smell the night on him. Stubble scratches my cheek, and his lips are almost at my ear, then he moves past me, too far, and gets himself another beer.

Christine Todd

Christine Todd grew up in County Durham, but spent most of her life in the American Midwest. She graduated from Concordia University–Wisconsin, and worked in radio advertising, most recently for ABC/Disney in Chicago. Her fiction has appeared in Leaf Books micro-fiction anthologies and *The Yellow Room* magazine. She and her husband now live in London. She writes a column for *Screentrade* magazine, and is completing her first novel and a collection of short stories.

Birdcage

Halfway through the roast duck, the fire bell shrieks. I panic. 'Shouldn't we be racing out of here?' I scan the dining room. Women in silk frocks and men in summer linens don't appear to have heard anything out of the ordinary. They sit straight-backed, their knives and forks busy.

Bill's right hand cuts through a swathe of air. 'Headlines in the British papers: "Honeymooning Yanks trample over Swan Hotel diners during fire drill."'

A waiter stops to refill our wine glasses. I call out over the din. 'What's happening?'

'We have an *awfully* small fire in the kitchen, Madam. I shouldn't worry.'

Anglophile Bill mops his mouth to hide his grin. I bet he's already formulating a British understatement story for our friends and family in Boston. They'll love it. 'Good thing we didn't act like chickens,' he chirps.

The alarm goes silent. Craning my neck toward the windows, I see the fire brigade has arrived. Hoses are being unrolled along the hallway past the dining room's open French doors. The alarm screams and is shut down, fast. Feathers unruffled, the locals dine on.

I mutter, 'Headlines in the British papers: "Tardy Yanks sizzle like Kentucky Fried Chicken during Swan Hotel blaze."'

'If flying the coop during one's evening meal is considered rude, our goose is already cooked,' says Bill, eyeballing the automatic kitchen doors as they open and close willy-nilly.

My stomach tightens. 'We're chicken if we run and we're chicken if we stay.'

He nods, serious for once. 'But when in Rome ... you know?'

We grimly clink glasses, gulp down our chilled Chardonnay, and peck at our roast duck. Even as we glimpse the dousing of kitchen flames, we don't budge from our perches.

Peter Meredith-Smith

Peter Meredith-Smith lives in Wales. On leaving school he trained as an actor, but never entered the profession. Instead, after short stints in various jobs (warehouseman, industrial painter & cleaner, roadie, assistant stage manager with an opera company, barman and oiler's mate), he set out on a career in mental healthcare. Today, he works as a government adviser on mental health issues. When not writing briefings and speeches for government ministers, Peter writes poetry, prose fiction and drama. In 2007 he completed a Bachelor of Arts Degree with the Open University, having majored in Literature Studies and Creative Writing.

A Thousand Coats

Gramps' house was owned by the colliery. The stones that made it came from the hill on which it stood.

It was limed – coated, here and there, with a brittle skin that could be picked away by curious hands to reveal the years gone by. In that hidden world, beneath those tree-ring layers, lived a multitude of tiny beasts: woodlice, millipedes, earwigs and spiders – as black as coal.

The house was two up: two down. Gramps and Nan had the front bedroom; the other was for the children. Downstairs could be found the back-kitchen and the front-parlour.

The kitchen's never-locked door led to a wonderland of brooks and trees and 'The Heap' at the top of the hill. The kitchen's heart was the range. It was huge, oily-black, iron-hot and homely. It was fed by coal dug by Gramps' own hands, and so it fed us with smoky chicken, golden-skinned rice puddings, roasted spuds and home-made bread.

The parlour was for the priest, suitors on their first visit and the deceased – before they departed the house on the hill for the last time. The parlour was my favourite room. It was secret and out of bounds. In that special place the chair was kept. Covered with oft-oiled leather, a million brass-topped nails punctuated its there-forever lines. I call it a chair because that's what the grown-ups said it was – though they seldom seemed to use it so. To them it was a place for coats – at times there seemed a thousand coats.

To me the chair was other things – known to me alone. To me it was a spaceship, a galleon on the Spanish Main, Scott's frozen tent beneath the snow or Tutankhamun's dusty tomb. To me it was a time machine.

Karen Jones

Karen Jones writes micro-fiction, short stories, comedy scripts and, occasionally, poetry (usually when someone or something has annoyed her). She is currently (and interminably) working on a novel. Thirty-two of her micro-stories are published in the Guidhall Press book *The Wonderful World of Worders*. She has also been published in *Writers' Forum Magazine, Candis Magazine, Our Atticus* ezine and the Writers' Bureau website. She was short listed for the 2007 Asham Award.

Curiosity

She had a grape in her hair. He wasn't sure if it was supposed to be there – some sort of affectation. He wondered if he should mention it, just walk up and say, 'Excuse me, but do you know you have a grape in your hair?'

Well, it would be awkward, wouldn't it? If she didn't know, she would be embarrassed, would feel compelled to find and provide an explanation. Maybe she'd enlist his aid in grape retrieval. He really didn't want to get involved with a stranger's hair.

And if she did know it was there, he didn't want to get involved with any part of a woman who deliberately kept a grape in her hair.

She caught him staring. 'Hey, are you looking at my grape?'

He nodded, guiltily.

'Well, don't. A face like yours could bruise it.'

He lowered his head, swallowed the obvious question: 'You have red hair – why are you sporting a green grape?'

Sometimes, he decided, it's best not to ask.

Bad Apples

He mixed the paint again, knowing he'd get it right eventually. It shouldn't be so problematic; it was just a still life. People were difficult, so they said, but not for him. He could paint a person (he never used the word 'portrait') and show their whole life in the tilt of a head, the crook of an arm, the slump of a shoulder.

People were easy. While other artists starved, his work was sought after, commissioned; offers of patronage, and other, more interesting offers from female clients came daily.

He started again. The table was perfect; it looked well used, well cared for, a table that had been loved. The bowl was beautiful; he'd brought out the craftsmanship. It was no ordinary bowl; it represented the art of the potter. It represented art itself.

He dipped his brush into green and daubed, once more, at the troublesome shapes in the centre of the canvas.

Defeated, he threw his brush across the studio. It was no good: the bloody things still just looked like apples.

Ruth Harris

Almost ten years ago, Ruth Harris escaped to Brighton. She has an MPhil in Writing from the University of Glamorgan and has won prizes/been shortlisted in a number of short story competitions including The Lichfield Prize, The Fish, The Biscuit, Blinking Eye and The Asham. Publications include *The New Writer, New Welsh Review, Cadenza, The Fish Anthology, Quality Women's Fiction* and magazines too obscure to mention. Five of her micro stories appeared on the '50 beans 50 words' website and other online credits include eastoftheweb and espresso fiction. Ruth can be found in beach cafes scribbling feverishly in her notebook.

Green Fingers

Until your granddad died I never planted a thing. He was the gardener in this house. Down the garden all day long - conditioning the soil, planting his crops and digging the new season potatoes. And not just his veg.

I was allowed among the sweet peas, but only to cut a few stems for the kitchen table. He said they needed to be cut, made them flower. So that was all right. When you were little I'd take you down the garden path to count the crocuses. How many purple, how many orange? You knew not to touch them.

Your granddad left a verandah bursting with geraniums. I had to do something with them when he passed. In winter he'd keep the plants in the spare bedroom, spare them from the frost. So I did too. I've taken cuttings, dipped them in hormone rooting powder and each one in a nice fresh pot. It wouldn't have mattered if they died. He wasn't here to see me make a fool of myself. They've done really well. There now.

These days I'm forever with my hands in a pot of soil. I like the feel of the compost, the way it crumbles, the musty smell of it. Good enough to eat. The geraniums like it, too. All my cuttings have taken. I'm so pleased I've asked next door for a few of theirs and we've done a swap. The last time you came round you said how nice to have whites and pinks to break up all that scarlet. He did like his scarlet, your granddad.

Think of this. I'm 82 and it's taken me this long to realise I've got green fingers. Wonder what your granddad would say.

Mo Singh

Mo Singh was born in the East Midlands. An artist and writer, she began (publicly) experimenting with words whilst studying for a fine art degree. Having gradually shed a voluntary sector career she is now freer to devote more attention to her creativity. Mo writes performance pieces as well as fiction and has recently had some cartoons published. She is currently completing a novella and planning a novel.